prayer

in every Religion

Abdul Waheed

Prayer in every Religion

Abdul Waheed

CERTIFICATE OF PUBLISHING

We're proud to present this certificate of publishing to

Abdul Waheed

for successfully publishing

PRAYER IN EVERY RELIGION

on 20-01-2023

*"A writer's life and work are not a gift to mankind; **they're a necessity"** ~ Toni Morrison*

Dedication

This book is dedicated to the memory of my late father Haji Ubairdur Rahman (Munna) and younger brother Abdul Hameed. May God (Allah) give peace to his soul
 Aamen

Table of contents

Preface

Every religion has its own prayer for that God or Master, only such prayer leads to welfare of life, a very good prayer is sung by Lata Mangeshkar in a famous Bollywood movie Do Aankhen Barah Haath, which is very old and old. Famously, this is how a prayer runs in the curriculum in the old schools as well. A person may be less religious, but when he is in any trouble, he definitely prays to his God or Master, only then he gets the peace of satisfaction, this is the truth. There is a prayer for that master in every religion, an attempt has been made in this book to understand how that prayer has gone somewhere, please read it and if you have any other prayer in your knowledge, please inform. Thank you,

Yours - Abdul Waheed, Barabanki

Date-21/12/2022.

famous prayer in school syllabus

who made the sun and moon

who made the sun and moon

that made the stars shine

who scented the flowers

the one who made the birds chirp

who made the whole world

we sing the praises of that god

Bow down to him with love.

ऐ मालिक
तेरे बंदे हम

A famous Bollywood song (Prayer) sung by Lata Mangeshkar-

O Lord, we are your servants

be like this our karma

walk in righteousness and avoid evil

to die laughing

when faced with oppression

then you hold us

they do evil we do good

don't wish to change

Every step of love increased

And this illusion of enmity disappeared

Walk in righteousness...

it's getting dark

Your person is getting scared

Your person is getting scared

nothing is happening unconsciously

Looks like happiness

the sun is hiding

That breath in your light

the one who does the new moon

Move over Poonam Neki...

very weak man

There are millions missing

but you who are standing are kind

Earth stopped by your grace

you gave us birth

You will bear all our sorrows

Walk on goodness....

prayer of islam religion

Al-Fatihah 1:1-7

(1) In the name of Allah the Most Gracious and the Most Merciful.

(2) Praise be to Allah alone, the Lord of the worlds

(3) Very kind, very kind

(4) He is the master of the day of recompense

(5) We worship you and you seek help

(6) Guide us on the straight path

(7) On the path of those who have been blessed by you, who have not been subjected to wrath and have not gone astray

prayer of hinduism

Tat saviturvarenya. Bhargodevasya Dhimahi. धियो यो नः Prachodayat. (Rigveda 3,62,10)

Gayatri Dhyanam

mukta-vidrum-hem-neel dhavalachhayairmukhastrikshanai-

Ryuktamindu-nibaddha-ratnamukutan tattvarthavarnatmikam.

Gayatri Varada-भयः-ङकुश-कशाः शुभ्रं कपलं गुना।

Conch, Chakramatharvinduyugal Hastairvahanti Bhaje ॥

That is, whose faces are ecstatic with the sharp aura of gems like pearl, coral, gold, sapphire, and diamond. The jewel in the form of moon is attached to his crown. Which are of characters that make you realize the element of self. We meditate on Gayatri Devi, who is holding the goad, abhaya, whip, kapal, veena, conch, chakra, lotus in both her hands with Varad Mudra.(Dr. Ram Milan Mishra)

Gayatri Mahamantra

Om Bhur Bhuva: Self.

Tat saviturvarenya.

Bhargo Devasya Dhimahi.

Dhiyo yo nahi prachodayat ||

Meaning -

Let us imbibe that soul in the form of life, the destroyer of sorrows, the embodiment of happiness, the best, the effulgent, the destroyer of sin, the divine. May that God inspire our intellect in the right path.

Na tatra sun bhati na chandratarakam nema vidyutyo bhanti kuto ayamagnih. Tamev Bhantamanubhati Sarvam Tasya Bhasa Sarvamidam Vibhati || There the sun does not shine, neither the moon nor the stars, nor even those lightnings, what to speak of fire, it only shines, everyone becomes resplendent by its radiance, it is its aura that enlightens all. publishes it. (Kathopanishad 5-15)

buddhist prayer

Sachittapariyodapanam and Buddhana Sasanam. To avoid all sins, to increase well-being, to keep one's mind pure, this is the teaching of the Buddha.

Prayer for the welfare of all living beings

Sabbe satta sukhi hotuntu, sabbe hotuntu cha khemino, sabbe bhadrani passantu, ma kacchi dukhmagma. "May all beings be happy and live well, may all take care of their own well-being and may no one suffer any sorrow. ,

jain prayer

Jah te na piyam dukkham tahev tesi pi jaan jeevanam. And Gachcha Appovamishro Jeevesu Hohi Sada || जीववहो अप्वावहो जीव दिया होदी श्रप्सनो हुदया। Visankatkovya violence should be avoided. Shray Tule Payasu, Mettin Bhusukappaye. Samvapana na holiyanva na nidiyava || Just as you don't want sorrow, similarly all the beloved creatures also don't want sorrow. Keeping this in mind, treat others the way you want others to treat you. To kill a living being is to commit suicide and to have mercy on all living beings is to have mercy on oneself. Therefore stay away from violence in the same way as one stays away from poison or thorn. Treat all living beings as yourself. Be a minister to all living beings. Do not insult anyone and do not criticize anyone.

Prayer for Enlightenment :-

I bow down to Lord Jinendra who has conquered fear, all troubles, sorrows, sensual pains, lust, passions, attachments, greed and attachment and pleasure and pain. May my sorrows be relieved and I may be completely freed from the bondage of karma. May I attain enlightenment and may my death be peaceful. Oh God Jinendra, who does welfare of all living beings! May I find shelter, pleasant refuge at your feet!

sikhism prayer

prayer for courage

Dehu Shiva bar mohi hai shubh karman te kabahu na taroon. Don't be afraid, when you die, win your victory with confidence. Are you a Sikh, your own mind is greedy for this victory. When the incoming weapon becomes a diagnosis, then fight and die in every run.

Jewish prayer

The earth and all that is in it is Jehovah, the world and those who live in it; For, it is he who has established its foundation over the seas, and established it over the rivers, who can climb the mountain of the Lord? And who can stand in his holy place?

Whose deeds are blameless, whose heart is pure, who does not turn his mind to vanity, and who does not swear falsely, he will be blessed by the Lord and righteous by the God of his salvation. ,

Taste and see how good the Lord is. Blessed is the man who takes refuge in him. Fear the Lord, you holy people. X X X "Keep your tongue from evil, guard your mouth that no deceit may come out of it; Leave evil and do good, find peace and follow it. The eyes of the Lord are on those who do righteousness. ,

Taoist Prayer

The greatest emphasis in Taoism is on Tao. How is that Tao?

The great Tao is omnipresent. He is on this side as well as on that side. All living beings live by that. He keeps on taking everyone's search and news. He does the work as well, he also completes the same. But, not even touching its fruit. He wraps everyone around with love. He nourishes everyone with love. But he doesn't even let the smell of superiority come in him. He has no ambition. No desire.

Where is Tao Teh King

1.   Tao The one who comes to say 'Tao' from the inexplicable Vanos, is not really 'Tao'. (Tao is a matter of experience, not of saying.) The quality that can be named is not its true characteristic. What was before earth and heaven is 'unmanifested'. ' Infinite and eternal Tao is infinite. Everything is born out of his ignorance. He makes round things round. He creates order through mixing and matching. He dazzles the shining thing with his brilliance. He is detached. No one knows from whom he was born. He is older than God. Unacceptable and

unthinkable Tao is unacceptable. It cannot be accepted. Tao is inconceivable. He cannot think properly. To follow that unapproachable and inconceivable Tao is the great religion. It is inconceivable, inconceivable, yet it has form. He is inconceivable, inconceivable, yet all things are included in him. 1 , 2. Tao Upanishad 1; 4.
He is from time immemorial, yet his nature is the same. He is the original cause of all things. how do i know him From Tao I get to know him. ,

  The nameless and simple axiom Tao is nameless. He doesn't have any name. Its fundamental simplicity is simple, yet the world does not imagine meanness in it.

  He will go on avoiding praise from a distance. He will cut the root of respect. As valleys are to the sea and rivers, so is Tao to the world. Absolute is this, absolute is that great Tao that is all-pervading. At the same time he lives on this side, on the other side as well. All living beings live because of him. He takes everyone's search - news. That's what works. He alone reaches to perfection. He doesn't even touch the fruit. He nourishes everyone with love. In doing so, he does not even allow the smell of superiority to enter. He doesn't have ambition, doesn't have any kind of desire 12 If he listens, he follows him.

universal prayer

O Lord of all religions, O Protector of the whole world. Oh soul - the great bundle of power, the father of the world, the controller of the world. Give us the courage of Vedavrat, give us the great wisdom of Buddha, give us the love of Jesus, give us the faith of Muhammad, Confucius, Tamro, Mahavir Zarathustra, Moses, Nanak, Kabir. Let us meditate, promote, spread the word of mouth, which is said by Pir. We respect Gita, Bible, Quran, Shrampad. Guru Granth, Tripitaka, Avesta of every religion and every religion. Parsi Bahai Buddhist Jain Hindu Muslim Sikh Christian. Ho sarva dharma equanimity Saras Manav Human are all brothers. Dr. Dauji

Prayer of Zarathushtra (Zoroastrian, Zoroastrianism)

Asham bahu vahishtem prasti usta asti usta grhamaya hayat ashai dahistai prabh. The best auspicious Asha is praised, it is the greatest happiness, he who follows Asha is always happy for the same. Kshnarth rahe Majdashro nemsete prat Majdashro Ahurahe Hudhaao Majist Yajat. Our praise to Ahura Mazda is (our) salutations to you, O Agni (Atar) of Ahura Mazda, you are the Beneficent and the Supreme Soul.

christian prayer

In the name of the Father and the Son and the Holy Spirit. Amen . ,

O our Father in heaven, may your name be sanctified, may your kingdom come, may your will be done on earth as it is in heaven. Give us our daily bread today, and forgive us our sins as we forgive our offenders, and do not tempt us but deliver us from evil, Amen. Glory be to the Father, the Son and the Holy Spirit as it was in the beginning, is now and will be forever, Amen. ,

Baha'i Prayer:

I bear witness, my God, that you have created me to know and worship you. At this moment, I am witness to my powerlessness and your power, my poverty and your prosperity. There is no other God except you, you are the helper in troubles, self-living. -- Baha'u'llah

prayers for unity

1 O my Lord, my God! Unite the hearts of your servants, and reveal to them the noble purpose. Give such a boon that they can follow your orders and follow your rules. O Lord, help them in their endeavours, and give them enough strength to serve You.

Hey Ish! Do not leave them helpless but guide them with the light of knowledge, and fill their hearts with your love. In fact, you are their helper and master. - Baha'u'llah 2 Kind hearted Swami! You have created the entire human race from a single element. According to your order, all are members of the same family. They are servants before you and the entire human race takes refuge under your great wisdom. All have gathered under the seat of Your grace and are illumined by the light of Your radiance.

O Lord, You are kind to all, You are the Sustainer of all, You give shelter to all, and You give life to all. You have given talent and morale to everyone, and everyone merges in the ocean of your Yada. Do it, O merciful Lord! Tie everyone in the thread of unity, establish agreement among religions and unite all words so that one house can be formed. May they become like one family and give such a boon to the whole earth that all may live in harmony and unity. Oh Lord, raise the flag of unity in mankind. O God unite the human hearts together. Ullasit - O merciful Lord, O Supreme Father, fill our hearts with joy with Your love, enlighten our eyes with the light of Your guidance, give joy to our ears with Your sweet voice, and give us shelter in the canopy. You are strong, mighty. You are forgiving and indifferent to the faults of mankind. -Abdul Baha

O king of humility! Resident of the inferior cottage of Deen Bhangi! Help us to find you everywhere in this beautiful land watered by the waters of the Ganges, the Yamuna and the Brahmaputra; give us receptivity and an open heart; Give your own humility; Give me the strength and eagerness to unite with the people of India. O God! You also come to help, when man takes refuge in You, becoming empty. Give us a boon that as a servant and a friend of the people whose We want to serve, never get separated from it. Make us an idol of sacrifice, humility, devotion and humility, so that, we can serve this country more. understand and want more.

(Mahatma Gandhi)

Prayer of the Druze religion

"On the concept of God, Hamza ibn Ali wrote

If human minds are given the knowledge of God without any introduction and order, those human minds will faint and fall.

...the originator of the perfect intellect. He virtually bound all created beings within it, so that there is nothing outside of it.

On the concept of reincarnation and the universal soul, Bahauddin wrote

O you who are distracted, how can he who is devoid of his material means, attain knowledge?

O you who are careless, how can he who renounces his sensual capacity, attain ignorance?

And O you who are confused, how can souls exist on their own?

And how can they dwell in their origin, and yet live life and attain their pleasures?

On the concept of atheism, Bahauddin argued

To believe in non-existence is to deny existence. It is a path that leads to disbelief Regarding the secrecy of the letters of knowledge, Hamza ibn Ali wrote

Protect the Divine knowledge from those who do not deserve it and do not withhold it from those who deserve it.

Whoever withholds Divine knowledge from those who deserve it will indeed be disrespecting what has been entrusted to him and committing sacrilege against his religion;

And whoever communicates it to those who do not deserve it will have his faith deviate from following the truth.

Therefore the scripture should be protected from those who do not deserve it.

However he commented

Protect yourself from ignorance with the help of the knowledge of the Oneness of our Lord...

Regarding the knowledge of the Oneness of God and of being in a state of peace of mind and contentment (rida') and of true love, Hamza ibn Ali left the message

I order you to protect your companions. In protecting them your faith reaches perfection."

Gnostic Prayer

Morning Prayer

In the name of the Father, the Son, and the Holy Spirit. Amen.

Upon awakening, Heavenly Father, I sing your praise and I dare to ask you again with faith to say the prayer that the Divine Master taught us.

Our Father who art in the depths of the ages, may your holy Logos and Christ be understood and worshiped throughout the universe; may the kingdom of your Holy Spirit come to us, may your will be done on earth as it is in heaven. Give us today our spiritual food, the strength and courage to earn bread for our bodies. Forgive us for deviating from your rules, just as our assembly forgives repentant sinners. Support us in our weakness so that we are not carried away by our passions and protect us from the deceptive mirages of the Archons. For we have no other King than your beloved Son Christ our Savior, whose kingdom, victory, and glory are forever. Amen.

O Lord, O divine Evangelist, hear my prayer, listen to my prayer; Let me hear the voice of your mercy from the very morning, for it is in your hands that I entrust myself. I worship you, I praise you, I give thanks to you from the very morning.

I thank you that you protected me during the night from all dangers and all evils that could harm me and from which you have covered me with your protection. During this day, remain my support, my strength, my refuge, my salvation and my consolation. Amen.

My Father, I thank you for all the good things I have received from you so far. It is the effect of your goodness that I am seeing this day; I want to use it to serve you. I dedicate all my thoughts, words, deeds and sufferings to you. Bless them, my God, so that there is no one who is not energized by your love and who does not give you glory. Amen.

In the name of the Father, the Son and the Holy Spirit. Amen.

Mandaean prayer

Instruction of Adam by Uthra

Do not slumber and do not sleep,

And do not forget what your Lord has commanded you.

House, do not be a son of the world,

And do not be named as a guilty person in Tibyl.

Do not love fragrant wreaths,

And do not love a seductive woman.

Do not love fragrance,

And do not neglect the night prayer.

Do not love treacherous spirits and seductive prostitutes. Do not love lust and false apparitions. Do not drink wine and do not be drunk and do not forget your Lord in your thoughts. Be careful in your coming and going Do not forget your Lord. Be careful in your coming and going Do not forget your Lord. Be careful in your sitting and standing Do not forget your Lord. Be careful in your resting and lying down Do not forget your Lord. Do not say that I am the firstborn, I am safe from foolishness in everything I do. Adam, look at the world which is a completely unreal thing. It is an unreal thing, which you cannot trust. (From the Ginza Rba, see also Hans Jonas, The Gnostic Religion, p. 84 n. 32)

The Nestorian Prayer

Translation from the Aramaic by M.J. Birney

By the power of our Lord Jesus Christ we begin to write

The Order of the Sanctification of the Apostles

which was composed by

Mar Addai and Mar Mari, blessed apostles

Our Lord, help me in your mercy, Amen

First

The priest begins: In the name of the Father, and of the Son, and of the Holy Spirit forever. Repeat three times glory to God on high, and peace on earth and a good hope to men forever and ever, Amen.

And then Our Father in heaven, hallowed be your name. Your kingdom come. Holy, holy, you are holy, our Father in heaven, for heaven and earth are filled with the splendor of your glory. Angels and men call out to you, Holy, holy, you are holy. Our Father in heaven, hallowed be your name. Your kingdom come. Your will be done on earth as it is in heaven. Give us today our necessary bread, and forgive us our debts, as we forgive our debtors. And do not lead us into temptation, but deliver us from the evil one. For Thine is the kingdom, and the power, and the glory, for ever and ever, amen. Glory be to the Father, and to the Son, and to the Holy Spirit, from everlasting to everlasting, amen and amen. Hallowed be Thy name, our Father in heaven. Thy kingdom come. Holy, holy, holy are Thou, our Father in heaven, on Sundays and feast days:

Our Lord and our God, in Thy mercy strengthen us in our weakness, that we may administer the Holy Mysteries, which are given unto Thee for the renewal and salvation of our feeble nature, through the mercy of Thy beloved Son, O Lord of all, the Father, the Son, and the Holy Spirit, for everlasting.Second, for the Lord's feasts: Our Lord and our God, give strength to those who truly believe in Your name, and who truly confess without perversion, that they may faithfully administer the forgiving Mysteries, which sanctify their souls and bodies. May they serve You reverently with hearts and minds cleansed from stain and from profane thoughts. May they glorify You continually for the salvation which You have bestowed upon us in the abundant mercy of Your grace forever, O Lord of all, Father, Son, and Holy Spirit. And they begin the appointed Mystery, and then: Peace be with us.

For memorials and ordinary days: May the venerable and illustrious name of Your glorious Trinity be worshiped, praised, honored, glorified, confessed, and blessed at every hour in heaven and on earth, O Lord of all, Father, Son, and Holy Spirit forever.

Prayers before the canticle

For Sunday: O my Lord, before the glorious throne of your majesty, and the high and lofty chair of your honor, and the awesome judgment seat of the sternness of your love, and the forgiveness altar established at your instruction, and the dwelling place of your glory, we, your people and the sheep of your pasture, together with the thousands of cherubs who glorify you, and the tens of thousands of seraphim and archangels who serve you, bow down, worship, confess, and glorify you at every hour, O Lord of all, Father, Son, and Holy Spirit forever.Second, for feasts of the Lord, by Mar Elia III, Catholicos: Before the awesome judgment seat of your majesty, and the lofty throne of your divinity, and the graceful chair of your honor, and the glorious place of your dominion, where those who serve you, the cherubs, sing praises ceaselessly, and those who glorify you, the seraphim, sing holy songs without ceasing, we bow down without fear Mare bow down, worship with trembling, and confess and glorify at every hour without ceasing, O Lord of all, the Father, the Son, and the Holy Spirit forever.

For memorials: The great, terrible, holy, blessed, gracious, and incomprehensible name of your glorious Trinity, and your grace to our race, we are obliged to confess, worship, and glorify at every hour, O Lord of all, the Father, the Son, and the Holy Spirit forever.

Then they say the appointed anthem of Kanke.(When the presbyter goes out, with the cross on his hands, and he ascends the bema, a deacon says: Peace be with us.)

Lakhumara's Prayer for Sundays and Feasts: O Lord and our God, when the pleasant aroma of the fragrance of your love spreads over us, and our souls are enlightened with the knowledge of your truth, may we be deemed worthy to receive the revelation of your beloved from heaven, and there we shall confess and glorify you without ceasing, in your crowned Church, filled with all help and all blessings, for you are the Lord and Creator of all, Father, Son, and Holy Spirit forever.

For Memorials: For all the helps and graces you have done towards us, which we are unable to repay, we shall confess and glorify you without ceasing, in your crowned Church, filled with all help and blessings, for you are the Lord and Creator of all, Father, Son, and Holy Spirit forever.

(For the offering of incense: In the revered and radiant name of the glorious Trinity may this incense which we offer be blessed for your honor, and may it be for our forgiveness, O Maker of pleasant roots and sweet spices, O

Lord of all, Father, Son, and Holy Spirit forever.)Then as a deacon carries the censer around: May Christ please you in His Kingdom, and may He accept your ministry in the goodness of His mercy. Amen.

And they continue: Lord, we confess and extol You, Jesus Christ, for You give life to our bodies and You are the Savior of our souls. - Lord, I have washed my hands thoroughly and have circled Your altar. Lord, we confess and extol You, Jesus Christ, for You give life to our bodies and You are the Savior of our souls. - Glory be to the Father, the Son, and the Holy Spirit, forever and ever, amen and amen. Lord, we confess and extol You, Jesus Christ, for You give life to our bodies and You are the Savior of our souls. -

A deacon: Let us pray. Peace be with us.

PRAYER: Truly, my Lord, You give life to our bodies; You are the good Savior of our souls and you constantly protect our lives. O my Lord, we are obliged to confess, worship and glorify You, the Lord of all, Father, Son and Holy Spirit, for ever and ever.

A Deacon: Raise your voices, all, and give glory to the living God.They answer: Holy God, Holy Mighty, Holy Immortal, have mercy on us. - Glory to the Father, Son, and Holy Spirit. Holy God, Holy Mighty, Holy Immortal, have mercy on us. From eternity to eternity, amen and amen. Holy God, Holy Mighty, Holy Immortal, have mercy on us. -

Prayer before the text: You who are holy, glorious, powerful, and immortal, who dwell in the saints and whose will is done, O my Lord, and have mercy on us and have mercy on us, as you are accustomed to do at every hour, O Lord of all, Father, Son, and Holy Spirit forever.

(When the reader of the text comes to the priest or the head of the priests, he blesses him and says: May the Lord God of all make you wise in His holy teaching, and may His mercy and compassion be upon the readers and those who hear. May you be a shining mirror for all who heed the word of teaching from your mouth and follow it, through the mercy of His mercy. Amen. And when the reader says: Bless me, my Lord. He blesses him in this way: God, the Lord of all, make you strong and wise in His holy teaching, through the mercy of His mercy. Amen.)

Then they read the text and add the appropriate shurya.

Prayer before the Apostle.

O Lord our God and our Lord, enlighten the impulses of our thoughts to us, so that we may heed and understand the sweet sound of Your life-giving and divine commands. Give us strength in Your grace and mercy to receive benefit from them - love, hope and salvation, which are useful to the soul and body. O Lord of all, Father, Son, and Holy Spirit, let us sing praise to You without ceasing at all hours.

But during memorials and fasts (except for fasting Sundays) they pray:O wise leader, wonderful overseer of your household and great treasures, abundantly providing every help and blessing in your mercy, we pray you, my Lord, and have mercy and have compassion on us as you do at every hour, O Lord of all, Father, Son, and Holy Spirit, forever.

Then they read the Apostle. And when the deacon who reads the Apostle says: Bless, my Lord. The priest replies: May Christ make you wise in his holy teaching, and make you a shining mirror to all who look to you.

Now when the priest descends from the bema and comes to the door of the altar, both he and the deacon bow down, and the deacon says: Let us pray. Peace be with us.

And the priest softly prays: You, radiance of your Father's glory and image of your Parent's essence, you who appeared and shone in the flesh of our humanity and enlightened rational beings with the knowledge of your greatness, O my Lord, enlighten our souls with the light of your Gospel, and allow us to meditate on your Scriptures. O Lord of all, Father, Son and Holy Spirit, may we forever lead to your life-giving and divine commandments.

(Reply to the singer when he says: Bless, O my Lord. The priest says to him: May God, Lord of all, confirm your thoughts and refine your singing, so that you may sing His praises through the goodness of His mercy. Amen.)When the priest goes to visit the Gospel: O Christ, light of the world and eternal life of all, hail the eternal mercy you send us. Amen.

When he picks it up to go out: Make us wise in your law and enlighten our thoughts with your wisdom. Sanctify our souls with your truth, and allow us to be obedient to your words and fulfill your commands at all times, O Lord of all, Father, Son and Holy Spirit, forever.

Second: O you who enlighten the rational with the knowledge of your greatness, O my Lord, enlighten my thoughts so that I may meditate on your holy and divine

Scriptures at all times, O Lord of all, Father, Son and Holy Spirit, forever.

For the incense: O my Lord, may the sweet fragrance that came from you when the sinful Mary anointed your head with perfumed oil mix with this incense which we offer in your honor and for the forgiveness of our debts and sins, O Lord of all, Father, Son and Holy Spirit, forever.

Church of Satan

Church of Satan, counterculture group founded in the United States in the 1960s by Anton Szandor Levy (1930–1997), born Howard Stanton Levy. Contrary to its name, the church did not promote "evil" but humanistic values.

The Church of Satan Wants You to Stop Calling These 'Satan-Worshipping' Alleged Killers Satanists (July 25, 2024)

A former carnival worker, Levy had absorbed a variety of occult and ritual-magic teachings over the years, which he incorporated into the tenets of the church he founded on Walpurgisnacht, or May Eve (April 30), 1966. His appearances on American television and other media coverage attracted early converts, though there were never more than a few thousand members at any given time. Reports of the colorful rituals held at LaVey's San Francisco home—which he painted black—kept the church in the news; several celebrities, including Jayne Mansfield and Sammy Davis, Jr., became associated with the church.

LaVey set forth the church's teachings and rituals in The Satanic Bible (1969). The church did not worship Satan as the embodiment of Christian evil or even as an existing being. Instead, LaVey taught that "his infernal glory" symbolized humanist values such as self-affirmation, rebellion against unjust authority, vital existence, and "unerring wisdom", LaVey's term for knowledge without error. Rituals were designed as psychodramas that encouraged members to develop their egos and leave behind their lives as submissive weaklings. Rituals included a Black Mass, in which a naked woman was used as an altar.During the early years of the church, Levy authorized the formation of local chapters or grottos throughout the United States. Several controversies occurred in the 1970s, including the defection of one of his key lieutenants, Michael Aquino, who founded the rival Temple of Set. In response to these controversies, Levy disbanded the grotto, but the church continued as a loose association of individual members connected to the national headquarters. In 1997, after Levy's death, Blanche Barton became the church's leader."

"The 20th century saw the rise of a number of new religions whose adherents called themselves Satanists or Luciferians, although their understanding of Satan or Lucifer as a person varied considerably. For example, some have insisted that they worship Lucifer, an entity they consider distinct from Satan, while others consider the two names synonymous with the same being. Modern religious Satanists can be roughly divided into two camps: atheists or rationalists, for whom Satan/Lucifer symbolizes the values they wish to support, and supernaturalists, who see Satan/Lucifer as a being who really exists and whom they wish to worship.

Religious Satanism owes much to the increasingly sympathetic reevaluation of Satan in the work of Romantic writers and artists in the early 19th century. For people such as Percy Bysshe Shelley, Lord Byron, and Victor Hugo, Satan was a heroic rebel who challenged arbitrary authority , and as such it was sometimes adopted as a symbol by left-wing and anticlerical groups (and several decades later by some rock musicians). This reevaluation led to the emergence of a number of religious groups that actively worshiped Satan or Lucifer during the first half of the 20th century, although such groups remained small and marginal even within occult circles.

The first major form of modern religious Satanism was the Church of Satan, founded in San Francisco in 1966 by Anton LaVey. LaVey also promoted his ideas through books, most notably The Satanic Bible (1969). LaVeyan Satanism was formally atheistic, presenting Satan not as a real being but as a symbol of humanity's animal nature. It nevertheless accepted some supernatural ideas, such as a belief in magic, with LaVeyan Satanists performing rituals with magical intent. LaVey's beliefs were inspired by right-wing libertarian principles and emphasized the idea that Satanists should regard themselves as an elite separate from the "herd" of normal humanity.

Satanism

An attendee at the Satan Temple's SatanCon wears a shirt that parodies the inspirational slogan "Live, Laugh, Love", Boston, April 28, 2023.

An alternative interpretation of religious Satanism was offered by the Temple of Satan (TST), founded in the United States in 2012. Sharing the Church of Satanism's claims that Satan does not exist, TST rejected Lévy's right-wing libertarian philosophy and embraced a left-wing progressive philosophy. TST became famous for stunts in defense of legal access to abortion and gay marriage, deliberately challenging the hegemonic role of Christianity in much of American society. Its members outlined a coherent worldview that emphasized bodily autonomy and the embracing of compassion, empathy, and reason, as well as performing rituals to mark major events in a person's life or to celebrate rebellion against unjust authority.

In contrast to these atheistic groups, there have been modern Satanists who consider Satan or Lucifer to be a real being. One of the first organized groups to take this stance, the Temple of Set, was formed in 1975 by Michael Aquino and other former members of LaVey's Church. Unlike the Church of Satan, Aquino's Temple held that Satan's true identity was Set, a deity derived from the ancient Egyptian pantheon, thus moving the organization away from its Satanic origins and toward modern Paganism. By the late 20th century, a growing number of people began to consider themselves theistic Satanists. These individuals were generally solitary practitioners, communicating with each other via the Internet rather than being members of a single church.

While organizations such as the Church of Satan and the Satanic Temple have embraced Satanism's transgressive image without endorsing criminal activity, other groups have moved into more radical territory. The best-known example is the Order of Nine Angles, which emerged in Britain in the 1970s. Although its occult teachings place comparatively little emphasis on Satan, the group describes itself as promoting "traditional Satanism." Endorsing human sacrifice, the order has called on its followers to join extreme political groups to further the disintegration of society. While a minor movement in its early decades, the Internet allowed the order to gain international influence among extreme right-wing networks in the 21st century.

"There are also individuals and small groups, often teenagers, who have declared themselves to be Satanists in order to project a criminal or rebellious image. These individuals sometimes engage in criminal behavior, including vandalizing churches, desecrating graves, and mutilating or killing animals. In some rare cases, such as the American serial killer Richard Ramirez and the Italian Beasts of Satan group, these self-proclaimed Satanists have also committed murder.

Kabirpanthi

Doctrines Kabirpanthi are followers of Kabir and his teachings. Kabir lived in the fifteenth century A.D. and was foremost among the sants or poet-saints. Kabir attempted to transcend the religious boundaries of North India and promote harmony between Hinduism, Islam and other non-Hindu religions. In this respect he was a forerunner of Ramakrishna and Gandhi. His eclectic faith centered on bhakti, devotion to God. Kabir was a master of the "inner religion," loving devotion to God who dwells in the heart. The names of God are Vaishnava, since Kabir's guru was Ramanand. But although Kabir often refers to Rama, Hari and "the name of Rama," he is using these to refer to the omnipresent reality that is beyond words and "beyond the beyond," identified with the void, the nothingness, or what Kabir calls the spontaneous, indescribable state. For Kabir the satguru, the perfect guru, is not Ramanand but the God speaking within the soul. Kabir's most important principle is the word. In Vaishnava teaching the shabda includes both divine inspiration and the word of the teacher. Kabir's teaching was entirely oral, with nothing in writing. The Kabirvani, the words of Kabir, were written down after his life and the oldest dated written record is found in the Guru Granth of the Sikhs, compiled around 1604. There are two other undated versions of the Kabirvani, one compiled by the Dadupanthis of Rajasthan around 1600 and called the Kabir Granthavali, and the Bijak, a version popularized in Bihar even if not compiled by the Kabirpanthis. Sant Dharm was a religion of the heart, open to all. Many of the Sants were women and Kabir himself was a Shudra, the lowest caste. Kabir followed the Muslim prayer and Hajj, andRejected the external aspects of Hindu religion such as idol worship and pilgrimage. He deliberately chose not to die in his hometown of Banaras. Kabir attacked Brahmins and yogis, saw no virtue in asceticism, fasting and almsgiving, and he despised the six schools of Hindu philosophy. He did not accept any caste distinctions. Despite Kabir's opposition to sectarianism, a sect of his disciples and followers formed after his death. Modern Kabirpanthis consider themselves Hindus. Kabir is usually considered a Hindu himself. Like all religious movements, theory and practice have not kept up with the ideals of the original teacher. Neema, the wife of a weaver, found him as an infant floating on a lotus in a pond near Banaras. She and her husband, Niru, raised Kabir as their own child. Other legends tell of Kabir's wife, Loi, son, Kamal, and daughter, Kamaliya, all born miraculously. Niru and Nima belonged to the Julahas, a low caste of Muslim weavers, and Kabir worked all his life as a weaver near Benares. The Julahas were probably recent converts to Islam and it is not certain whether Kabir was circumcised. To them the Muslims were "Turks".Kabir's preachings appealed to the common intellect and were sarcastic and sharply worded and this caused hostility between Hindu and Muslim religious authorities. The legendary biography of Kabir details his persecution by the Muslim ruler Sikander Lodi, although Kabir eventually came to terms with him. The Brahmins attacked him for having an affair with a disreputable woman and for having a religious guru named Raidas, a Chamar, a leatherworker. Kabir (c. 1440-1518) is of great importance in the religious history of India. He was almost certainly a disciple of the Vaishnava bhakti teacher Ramanand (see Ramavatsa). There is a story of how a simple Muslim Julaha tries to become a disciple of Ramanand. One morning Kabir lay down on the ghat on the bank of the Ganges where Ramanand used to bathe, and on his way there he trampled Kabirand said "Rama,

Rama! What is this poor creature I have trampled upon?" Kabir considered "Rama, Rama!" as the mantra to become a disciple. Although Ramananda forgot this, when Kabir claimed before the people that he was a disciple, he called Kabir and hugged him to his chest, remembering the incident at the ghat. Kabir's teachings were the first significant introduction of Vaishnava bhakti to North India, and he was the first teacher to attract both Hindus and Muslims. His teachings were one of the main sources used by Guru Nanak, the founder of Sikhism. Kabir's eloquence was so powerful that his "words" spread like fire throughout North India, from Punjab and Rajasthan to Bihar. There is a famous legend about Kabir's death. He died in Maghar near Gorakhpur and a dispute arose between his Hindu and Muslim followers. The Hindus wanted to cremate him and the Muslims wanted to bury him. While they were arguing, Kabir appeared and told them to remove the cloth from his dead body. The body had disappeared and in its place was a heap of flowers. The Muslims took half of the flowers and buried them at Maghar and built a mausoleum at that place. The Hindus took their half of the flowers to Banaras and cremated those flowers at a place now known as Kabir Chaura, the name of a branch of the Kabirpanthis. The most authentic version of the Kabirvani was the Bijak, compiled by Bhago Das, an immediate disciple of Kabir. Bijak literally means invoice or account book. Other successors of Kabir wrote hymns, stotras and doctrinal poems which still exist in manuscript form at Kabir Chaura. Kabir was opposed to sectarianism and when the Kabirpanthis grew into a sect after his death, his son Kamal traditionally refused to lead them. Within a hundred years of Kabir's death, tradition says that the sect split into twelve sub-sects. One of these may have been the Udasi. Today only two sub-sects survive, the Kabir Chaura and the Dharmdasi. Dharam Das founded his own group in Chhattisgarh. He belonged to a Bania, the merchant caste, and Kabir rebuked them for their traditional image-worship.

Symbols   Although Kabir was strongly opposed to all external mechanical aspects of religion, he used symbolically many Vaishnava names of God to describe the omnipresent Reality.

The Kabirpanthis, however, still maintain monotheism and oppose image-worship. For Kabir the only Guru was the Satguru, but the Kabirpanthis are most careful in selecting the Guru, who must be followed throughout life. Members wear a garland of beads made of Tulsi wood, which is sacred to Lord Vishnu. A woman may wear it after marriage. Those belonging to the Dwij caste wear the sacred thread of Hinduism, the Janeu. There is an elaborate ceremony of initiation. The water is used to wash the feet of the Mahant, the Guru. The secret name of God is imprinted with dew on a betel leaf and it is called parwana, passport, which represents Kabir's body. The dew is collected in a vessel called amr and is water received directly from heaven. A secret mantra, the sacred utterance, is an important part of the ceremony. Dharamdasis use several mantras and their initiation ceremonies differ in some details. The ceremonies are conducted by a Mahant. Mahants receive authority from the head Mahant, who is Kabir's representative. Mahants have as symbols of authority a red cap, a black wool necklace called a seli, and a special rosary called a panch maal. At the time of appointment they offer a coconut, which has a special symbolic meaning for Kabirpanthis. The coconut has a face resembling a man, its surface is in three parts symbolizing Brahma, Vishnu, and Shiva, its flesh gradually decays to resemble human flesh, and it differs from other fruits because it does not contain seeds. Breaking the coconut is a bloodless sacrifice, an offering of peace to Niranjan (meaning "devoid of lusts," a title of God given by Kabirpanthis) for Kabirpanthis to obtain entry into heaven. The water in which the head Mahant's feet are washed becomes charan mitra, the amrit of feet (nectar of the gods). It is mixed with fine clay and made into tablets.and is swallowed or ground and mixed with water and drunk. Kabir Chaura Math is the place where Kabir traditionally instructed his disciples. The Math or monastery houses the Khanraon, a pair of wooden slippers representing Kabir's feet, and Kabir's pillow, the gaddi. On the walls of the Math are pictures of Kabir, Ramanand and the mahants. Above the pictures are designs in coloured cloth symbolising the five elements and the nine doors of the human body. Followers The 1901 census found 843,171 Kabirpanthis. Even today a large number of Kabirpanthis are concentrated in Banaras and extend to Gujarat in the west and Bihar in the east. Members are mainly low caste Hindus, with merchant castes playing an important role, especially among the Dharmdasis. The tradition of the saints is very influential through bhajans, devotional songs which have great appeal among Hindu communities in India and abroad. The headquarters/main centre is located at Kabir Chaura Banaras

Sarna Dharma Prayer

Jai Chala Yo, Jai Sarna Maa

1. (Jai Chala Yo, Jai Sarna Maa... 2, Chala Tonka Bara Lagadam)... 2 (Jai Chala Maa, Jai Sarna Maa, we are coming to the Sarna Sthal)

Jiya nu baray yo jayanti padom, kaya nu baray yo sachhe manti vignati nanom.... 2 (O Sarna Maa, come to my soul (heart), we will sing from our heart, come to my body, mother, we will plead with a true heart)

2. (Jai Chala Yo, Jai Sarna Maa... 2, Dharam Kudhiya Bara Lagadam)... 2 (Jai Chala Maa, Jai Sarna Maa, Dharam Kudhiya is coming)

Jiya nu baray yo jayanti padom, kaya nu baray yo sachhe manti vignati nanom.... 2 (O Sarna Maa, come to my soul (heart), we will sing from our heart, come to my body, mother, we will plead with a true heart We will make a request)

3. (Jai Chala Yo, Jai Sarna Maa...2, Lur Kudhiya Bara Lagdam)...2 (Jai Chala Maa, Jai Sarna Maa, Lur Kudhiya is coming)

Jiya nu baray yo jyanti padom, kaya nu baray yo true manti vinati nanom....2 (O Sarna Maa, come into my soul (heart), we will sing with all our heart, come into my body, mother, we will make a request with all our heart)

4. (Jai Chala Yo, Jai Sarna Maa...2, Akheda Bara Lagdam)...2 (Jai Chala Maa, Jai Sarna Maa, Akheda is coming)

Jiya nu baray yo jyanti padom, kaya nu baray yo true manti vinati nanom....2 (O Sarna Maa, come into my soul (heart), we will sing with all our heart, come into my body, mother, we will make a request with all our heart We will request and pray)

5. (Jai Chala Yo, Jai Sarna Maa...2, Jatra Tonka Bara Lagadam)...2 (Jai Chala Maa, Jai Sarna Maa, we are coming to the Jatra Sthal)

Jiya nu baray yo jyanti padom, kaya nu baray yo true manti pratyav nanom....2 (O Sarna Maa, come into my soul (heart), come into the body from the heart, mother, we will request and pray with a true heart)

We will sing, 6. (Jai Chala Yo, Jai Sarna Maa...2, Sirasita Bara Lagadam)...2 (Jai Chala Maa, Jai Sarna Maa, Sirasita we are coming)

Jiya nu baray yo jyanti padom, kaya nu baray yo true manti pratyav nanom....2 (O Sarna Maa, come into my soul (heart), we will sing from the heart, come into the body mother, we will request and pray with a true heart will request)

My another books

Sr no.	Book
1	World's Major religions, doctrines and sects
2	An introduction to the Holy Qur'an and it's unsolved mysteries
3	How did humans and language originate ?
4	Islam an introduction and sect
5	Sermons of great people
6	Prayer
7	Allah an introduction
8	Is Al khizr still alive today?
9	Story of harut and marut
10	Grief
11	The mysterious story of Al kahf (Ar raqim)
12	Naming of God

All these books are available in Hindi language and other international languages and are also available in e-book for **free on Google Play** Store.

My personal introduction

My name is Abdul Waheed, my father's name is Late Haji Ubaidur Rahman and mother's name is Jaibunnisa. I have liked scientific ideology since childhood and have a calm nature and attachment to books. Due to which my curiosity interest has been continuously used in new discoveries and information. I got selected in polytechnic while doing BSc, but unfortunately it remained incomplete because father and brother died. Two words of my father, which are very precious for my life, first - earn honestly, do not take support of lies, secondly, respect food and eat as much as you want. That's why the education remained incomplete due to the responsibility of the house, then later getting married. Still did not lose courage and today the book is available in front of you in the form of my thoughts. If any information is left incomplete, please let us know.

Thank you .